Sir Luke
the cat

Mesa Stradinger

Printed in the United States of America

ISBN: Softcover   978-1-63871-215-2
        eBook   978-1-63871-225-1

Republished by: PageTurner Press and Media LLC
Publication Date: 05/25/2021

To order copies of this book, contact:

PageTurner Press and Media
Phone: 1-888-447-9651
order@pageturner.us
www.pageturner.us

TO MY FIRST GRADE TEACHER, MRS. ASHCRAFT, WHO ALWAYS
SAID I WOULD BE AN AUTHOR.

TO MY DAD, LUKE, THE CLEANEST PERSON I KNOW.

TO MY MOM, KRYSTAL, WHO SHARES MY LOVE OF READING,
WRITING, AND WAS THE INSPIRATION FOR MY STORY.

Once upon a time, a long time ago, in a land far away, there lived a cat named Luke, who loved to be clean. He would brush his teeth after each meal.

Fun Facts: Did you know cats can get cavities just like people? These cavities are called resorptive lesions. Most of the time, people aren't aware their cats have cavities until they notice a missing tooth!

Luke would take a bath every Tuesday, Thursday, and Saturday.

Fun Facts: Did you know cats are naturally very clean. They spend 1/3 of their "awake" time in grooming. Cats use their tongues to bathe themselves. A cats tongue has special features called "papillae". They work the same way as a human hair brush.

Luke was the cleanest cat in all the land.

There was also a very dirty cat. He was the king's brother, and his name was Skunk. He was the dirtiest cat in all the land. His fur was black, and he had a white patch of hair on his head, just like a skunk. He liked to sleep in the garbage, and he never took a bath.

Fun Facts: Did you know that cats like to go through the garbage to find food to eat?

10

Skunk wanted to rule the kingdom. He planned to have his friends make a stink bomb filled with stinky stuff.

Skunk wanted to light the stink bomb inside the king's castle.

When the stink bomb went off in the castle, he thought everyone would run away because the smell would be so bad. After everyone left, Skunk thought he would rule the kingdom.

Fun Facts: Did you know there are 40 recognized different breeds of domestic cats in the world? The largest domestic cat breed is the Maine Coon. A group of cats is called a "clowder".

While Skunk was forming his plan to overtake the kingdom, Luke was at home taking a nap. He loved taking naps as much as he loved taking baths.

Fun Facts: Did you know a cat spends 16 to 20 hours per day napping? That means a cat spends 2/3 of its life sleeping.

The King heard of Skunk's plan to overthrow the kingdom, and he knew that the only cat that could stop skunk, was Luke. So the king sent his guards to bring Luke to the castle so that he could ask him for his help.

Fun Facts: Cats usually walk on all four legs, but they tend to sit or stand on their hind legs to look over at something, a bit like humans when we stand on our tip toes.

When Luke arrived at the castle he bowed to greet the king. "Rise Sir Luke", said the king. Luke was surprised to hear the king call him "Sir Luke". Luke replied, "I'm just plain Luke your majesty, not Sir Luke". "I have dubbed thee Sir Luke" said the king. "I have a very important job for you to do".

The King told Sir Luke about Skunk's plan to overthrow the kingdom. He asked Sir Luke to stop Skunk from igniting his stink bomb. In exchange for his services, the King promised to let Sir Luke marry his daughter, Princess Krystal.

As soon as Sir Luke saw Princess Krystal, he immediately fell in love, and agreed to help the king stop Skunk.

Sir Luke left the castle and ran as fast as he could to Skunk' secret hideout, the garbage disposal. He wanted to hurry, because he knew that as soon as he completed the mission that the king gave him, the sooner he could marry Princess Krystal.

Fun Facts: Did you know that a cat can travel at a top speed of approximately 31 mph over a short distance? A cat can also jump up to five times its own height in a single bound.

Sir Luke climbed up the back of the mountain behind the garbage disposal so that no one would see him coming. Sir Luke was exhausted when he found the secret entrance to the garbage disposal near the top of the mountain.

Fun Facts: climbing upward for cats, is instinctive, but they can't climb down face first because they're claws point the same direction. They can't get a good grip, so they have to back down really slow when climbing down.

Sir Luke crept through the secret entrance into the garbage disposal. He found Skunk fast asleep, laying in a pile of garbage, next to the stink bomb. Sir Luke quietly grabbed a bucket of water, and tip toed over to Skunk and...

...Sir Luke dumped the bucket of water on Skunk! This was Skunk's first bath, and the experience startled him so much, that he couldn't move at all. He was soaking wet!

Fun Facts: Cats hate getting wet! When a cat's fur gets completely drenched, they are weighed down and they are not as agile as when they are dry.

34

Quick as a wink, Sir Luke scooped Skunk up and stuffed him in a sack. Sir Luke ran out of the garbage disposal with Skunk slung over his shoulder. Just as Sir Luke was running out of the main entrance of the garbage disposal, the stink bomb accidentally went off! The smell was so bad, that the garbage disposal tumbled to the ground!

Sir Luke delivered Skunk to the king. The king kept his promise, and honored the marriage of Princess Krystal to Sir Luke. They were married that very day. Sir Luke had saved the kingdom from the stinky Skunk cat and his stink bomb. Sir Luke and Princess Krystal lived happily ever after.

Fun Facts: A cat's sense of smell is 14 times stronger than a human. A cat's entire nasal organ is bigger than a humans. Some smells that cats hate consist of lemons, limes, dirty litter boxes, cayenne pepper, and cat nip, to just name a few.

As for Skunk, well... the king sentenced him to a lifetime of baths every Tuesday, Thursday, and Saturday!

THE END

CPSIA information can be obtained
at www.ICGtesting.com
Printed in the USA
BVRC091226120721
611739BV00002B/14